W9-BLT-097

To my Libras, you know who you are.
With thanks to Amelia and Andrea.
—B. B.

Copyright © 2011 by Brigette Barrager.
All rights reserved. No part of this book may be reproduced in any form
without written permission from the publisher.

Library of Congress Cataloging-in-Publication Data
Barrager, Brigette.
Twelve dancing princesses / retold and illustrated by Brigette Barrager.
p. cm.
Summary: An easy retelling of the tale of twelve princesses who dance
secretly all night long and how their secret is eventually discovered.
ISBN 978-0-8118-7696-4
[1. Fairy tales. 2. Folklore—Germany.] I. Grimm, Wilhelm, 1786–1859. II.
Grimm, Jacob, 1785–1863. III. Zertanzten Schuhe. English. IV. Title.
PZ8.B258Twe 2011
398.2—dc22
{E}
2010011580

Book design by Amelia May Anderson.
Typeset in Bodoni Classic and LHF Quaker.
The illustrations in this book were rendered digitally.

Manufactured by Toppan Leefung, Da Ling Shan Town, Dongguan, China,
in January 2011.

1 3 5 7 9 10 8 6 4 2

This product conforms to CPSIA 2008.

Chronicle Books LLC
680 Second Street, San Francisco, California 94107

www.chroniclekids.com

Twelve Dancing Princesses

Retold and illustrated by
Brigette Barrager

chronicle books · san francisco

Once upon a time, in a kingdom far away, there were twelve princesses. Their names were Rose, Iris, Daisy, Tulip, Petunia, Bluebell, Clover, Violet, Zinnia, Lilac, Daffodil, and Poppy.

Each one was lovelier than the flower she was named for.

Although their lives were charmed, they had
developed a mysterious problem: Every morning,
without fail, the soles of the princesses' shoes
were worn out and full of holes.

And the princesses spent every day sleeping
in the palace garden, snoozing and lounging
like cats in the shade.

The King had to hire a cobbler especially
for the princesses. His name was Pip. He worked
day and night to make shoes fit for royalty.

Pip liked Princess Poppy because she always told him how beautiful the new shoes were.

"They are soooo . . ." she would say as she yawned, ". . . lovely, Pip!" And then she would fall asleep again, just like that. Poppy really liked Pip, too, but she just couldn't keep her eyes open long enough to say so.

The King soon became quite concerned with
the princesses' strange, sleepy habits.

"How can I expect my daughters to rule the
kingdom after me, when they spend their days
napping?" he thought.

So he made a proclamation: "Solve the mystery
of the sleepy princesses and you shall have any
treasure your heart desires, no matter how great."

Soon, all sorts of scientists, scholars, doctors, detectives, fortune-tellers, and philosophers arrived to lend their expertise.

They studied the princesses while they slept—or tried to sleep.

They inspected and inquired,

searched and
researched,

examined and explored.

Of course, all of this only made the
princesses wearier than ever!

The experts tried and tried to explain the mystery of the sleepy princesses and the worn-out shoes, but they could not.

"If the brightest and best minds in the kingdom cannot help us, who can?" the King sighed, and great sorrow fell over the court.

Only one person would not give up so easily: Pip!
He devised a plan to solve the mystery and went to
work immediately. That day he made himself a pair
of the softest, most silent shoes possible . . .

. . . and that night, after everyone had gone to bed and the castle was dark and still, Pip snuck to the princesses' room, put his ear to the door, and waited. Soon he heard a stirring, rustling, swooshing sound, but not a single word. Not even a whisper.

Pip peeked through the door and saw all twelve princesses dressed in their finest gowns. They looked as though they were going to a grand ball, but their eyes were still closed as if they were sleeping.

"Are they sleepwalkers?" wondered Pip.

But just then an extraordinary thing happened. A trapdoor appeared in the floor, and its doors swung wide open.

Inside were steep stairs leading down, down, down. The princesses descended one by one, still fast asleep. Pip crept along behind them, quieter than a mouse in his exceptional shoes.

The stairs led into a cavern filled with a
forest of shimmering, shining, glittering trees
made of silver, gold, and diamonds. Perched
in the trees were beautiful jewel-colored birds,
singing quiet lullabies.

"This is a magic place,"
thought Pip. "No one would
believe it unless they saw it!"
So he broke a few twigs off
the trees, to keep as proof.

At the edge of the forest was a dark, dreamy
lake with boats waiting on its shore.

The princesses stepped aboard, and Pip had to jump on quickly before they began to float silently toward an island.

"This is definitely some kind of enchantment," thought Pip.

On the island was a ballroom, with candles flickering and music playing. The princesses began to dance, twirling and turning, dipping and bowing, graceful as ballerinas.

"No wonder their shoes wear out every night!" thought Pip.

The princesses danced
for hours and hours, until
morning. Suddenly the music
faded, and just as quietly as
they had arrived the princesses
left the island.

"I can't let this continue,"
said Pip.

He had read enough stories
to know that kisses are almost
always the best antidote for
spells, but he was so much of
a gentleman that he could only
bring himself to kiss Poppy's
delicate hand.

No sooner had he done so
than her eyes fluttered open,
and so did all her sisters' eyes.

Before anyone could utter a word, the forest
of silver and gold and diamonds began to crumble
into vapor and dust.

The princesses hurried up the stairs and into
the room where the trapdoor slammed shut and
disappeared in a whirl of smoke.

"What happened?" asked Rose, rubbing her eyes.

"Why are we all dressed up?" yawned Zinnia.

"You were under a spell, Your Highnesses," explained Pip. "You traveled to an underground land and danced all night. I followed you there and . . ."

". . . and you broke the spell?" asked Poppy, who was quite happy to see Pip.

"Yes, I suppose I did," said Pip.

"Let's go tell Father that the mystery is solved!" she exclaimed.

They rushed to the throne room to give the King the good news, and Pip told the whole story.

"Do you have proof that this underground land existed?" asked the King.

Pip took the silver, gold, and diamond twigs from his pocket. They sparkled in the daylight.

"I knew there was still magic stirring in these castle walls," said the King.

"You were more clever and brave than all the wisest people in the kingdom put together, and you have saved my daughters from their enchantment! So what reward do you choose? One thousand bags of gold? A chest of diamonds? A castle of your own? What is your heart's desire?" asked the King.

"Your . . . Your Majesty, more than anything else I'd like to ask for Poppy's hand in marriage," answered Pip nervously.

Poppy smiled brightly. "Yes!" she said, "yes, of course!"

From that day on, the princesses were happy and lively, and they never spent another day snoozing in the garden.

Pip and Poppy were married, and at their wedding, the princesses danced more beautifully and joyfully than they ever had before.

And, of course, they all lived happily ever after.